KB005705

여기 그대 곁에

나 언제나 있었는데

I have always been here beside you

여기 그대 곁에

펴낸곳 (주)도어스
지은이 강영희
그린이 이성표
디자인 조의환
펴낸이 김동규
초판1쇄 2016년 12월 15일
주소 03169 서울 종로구 사직로10길 7(내자동)
전화 070-4231-4232
Facebook 강영희
Twitter @gumunjadab
Instagram kang_younghee_love
홈페이지 9moon.co.kr
등록번호 2016년 5월 12일 제300-2016-54호
ISBN 979-11-958208-2-5
값 13,000원

여기 그대 곁에 나 언제나 있었는데
I have always been here beside you

강영희 글 | 이성표 그림

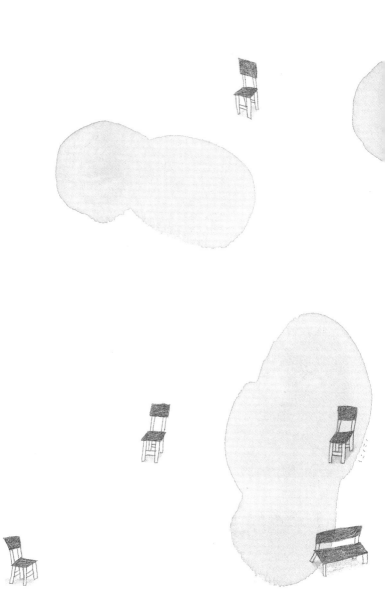

Translation

Mi Na Sketchley
Korean Translator & Conference Interpreter
MA MCIL DPSI Korean (English Law) NRPSI
Reading for DPhil Oriental Studies, Oriental Studies
Faculty, University of Oxford

Anthony Charles E. Banks
Editor and proofreader. ESL professional
University of London

Hyangkue Lee
Independent Researcher, Writer and Translator
PhD. Education, Seoul National University

차례 Contents

하루

a day

하루가 너무 짧아요

당신이 제 안에 드리우신 햇살이

굽이굽이 너무 길어서요

A day is too short

because the sunshine you spread inside me

swirls about and lasts far too long.

하루
a day

1-1

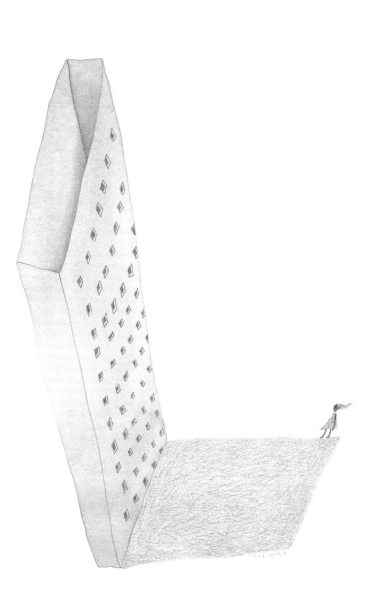

There was an unripe green persimmon hanging on a tree

I painted it with the dark red-orange colour that I found while rummaging around inside my head

The persimmon tree now bears Autumn

Too soon!-so I wipe the painted colour off

But still!–I engrave the colour from the palette onto my heart

The joy of waiting is the most precious gift you have ever given me.

감나무에 파란 땡감이 달렸네
머릿속을 뒤져 감색 물감을 찾아 땡감에 칠을 했어
감나무에 가을에 열렸네
'아직은'이라서 물감을 지웠고
'그래도'이기에 팔레트의 물감을 가슴에 담았어
기다리는 즐거움은 당신이 내게 주신 최고의 선물이었어

돌아보았어요 어떻게 해서 당신을 사랑하게 되었는지를
모든 생각이 사라진 자리에 당신 얼굴만 하얗게 보이더군요
그곳으로 뛰어갔어요
돌아올 수 없는 그곳으로 저도 모르게 날아갔어요
오직 당신만 계신 그곳으로 영원히 사라졌어요

I look back to figure out how I fell in love with you
In the empty space after all thoughts have disappeared,
only your face remains, shrouded in white
I ran towards it
Without a second thought, I flew to the place where I could not return
I have vanished into the place where only you exist.

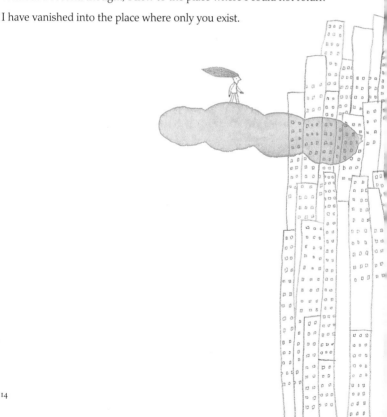

하루
a day
1-3

텅 빈 바구니

the empty vessel

새앙쥐가 자라는 이빨을 갈아내듯

우리는 넘치는 사랑을 비워내야 해요

당신이 그걸 알려주셨어요

두려운 마음으로 발 동동 구르던 저에게 비우는 방법을 가르쳐주셨어요

텅 빈 바구니에 당신의 향기가 가득하네요

Just like a tiny door mouse grinds his teeth,

we need to learn how to empty our overflowing love

You are the one who told me that

You are the one who taught me what to do while I was so riddled with fear

The empty vessel is now full of your scent.

어느날 당신이 오셔서 가슴속 돌덩이를 치워주셨어요

텅 빈 자리에 당신을 모시고 싶어요

당신을 모시려면 돌덩이 따위 더는 들여놓지 말아야 겠어요

자취 없이 다녀가시는 햇살 같은 당신을 기다리는

작은 공터가 되고 싶어요

One day, you came to me and cleared away a stone from my heart

I would love to invite you into the empty space thus created

To welcome you, I shall never again let any stones rest in my heart

You are so much like sunshine; it comes and goes with no trace left behind

I want to become a small vacant space, waiting for you.

가을에 태어나 가을만 살다가

가을에 죽어도 좋겠어

겨울이 오기 전 자취를 감추는 덧없는 평생이이도 좋겠어

사랑도 그랬으면 좋겠어

뜨겁지도 차갑지도 않은 사랑

시원한 갈바람에 바보같이 웃고 있는 당신 모습처럼

속절없는 사랑이어도 좋겠어

I wouldn't mind being born in autumn,

to live for just a single autumn and then pass away

I wouldn't mind a fleeting life that vanishes without a trace before the winter arrive

I would like love to be like this too

A love that is not too hot nor too cold

I wouldn't mind a futile kind of love, just like the love you had

with that fool smiling naively in the cool autumn breeze.

꽃들의 말을 엿들었어

꽃이라고 꽃다운 말만 하는 건 아니었어

삐죽거리며 흉을 보고 있더라니까

꽃도 아니면서 자기들이 꽃인 줄 아나봐

별꼴이 반쪽이야

인간들 얘기였어

하마터면 나도 따라 흉을 볼 뻔 했다니까

나도 내가 꽃인 줄 알았나봐

I overheard the flowers chatting

I realised that flowers don't always say flowery things

They could be churlish and foul-mouthed

"They think they are flowers but they are most certainly not!"

"It's terrible!"

They were talking about humankind

I was so close to joining in their sullen gossip

I must have thought I was a flower too.

Choo-choo… I want to take a train to somewhere far away

Don't we all have that moment?

The moment when I need to find you, you have the face of a stranger,

in that village far away over the mountain

The moment when the brooks, each with their own pasts,

crash into each other while waiting to merge into one, getting ready to run

Isn't there a moment when even love needs to be looked back at from a distance?

기차를 타고 빠앙 먼 곳으로 떠나고 싶어

그래야 할 때가 있잖아

산 너머 마을에 낯선 얼굴로 계신

당신을 찾아가야 할 때

저마다 달려온 냇물이

우당퉁탕 하나되어 흘러갈 순간을 기다리며

사랑도 그렇게 멀리서 되짚어 와야 할 때가 있잖아

김광석(1964–1996)

한국의 인기 가수. 그룹 <동물원>의 멤버이자, <노래를 찾는 사람들>의 창단 멤버.
나중에 솔로로 독립함. <먼지가 되어>는 1976년에 창작된 발라드 대중가요로,
1996년 김광석이 편곡하여 불러서 대중에게 널리 알려졌다. 사인(死因)에 의문을 남기고,
서른세 살에 요절하였다.

Kim Kwang-Seok(1964–1996)

A famous Korean singer, *Kim Kwang-Seok* was a member of a Korean band, *Dong-Mool-Won; Zoo*. He was also a founding member of a Korean band, *No-Rae-Rul Chan-Nun Sa-Ram-Duel; People Looking For Songs*. He later pursued a solo career. *'Becoming (Light) Dust'* is a ballad pop song, released in 1976, which *Kim Kwang-Seok* arranged in 1996 and is widely loved by the Korean public. He died young at 33 with several question marks over the cause of his death.

작은 가슴 모두 모두어

시를 써봐도 모자란 당신

먼지가 되어 날아가야지

바람에 날려

당신 곁으로

다시 또 먼지되어

당신 곁으로 가리라

눈물조차 버무려 주먹밥 먼지되어

이제는 두근두근 기쁨의 먼지되어

-tribute to 김광석

I don't have enough of you even though I try to write a poem

with each and every piece of my heart

I shall become light dust

blown away by the wind

drift to you

I shall become light dust again

drift to you

I shall even mix my tears into dust, form dust like a rice ball

I shall become a pitter-patter dust of delight

-tribute to *Kim, Kwang-seok,* singer

바람이 되어

날아가요

흐느적 몸이 구부러져요

바람 가락에 실려 라일라일 춤추어요

흐물흐물 물기가 돌아요

하늘에서 비를 쏟으시려나

뚜욱 눈물이 떨어지려나

흐읍 콧물이 나오려나

어쩌다보니 허공에서 잠들었어요

Becoming like wind

I am flying

My wobbly body is bending

dancing with swaying arms

mushy, pulpy, moist air swirls around me

Is the sky going to pour out her rain?

Tum, is the tear going to drop?

Hoope, is my nose running?

Up there in the air, I drift into sleep.

하얀 나비 한 마리가 날아가요

하얀 장갑을 끼고 나비를 잡아요

후우후우

나비를 책 속에 넣어요

넓다란 책 속에 들어간 나비는 하얀 광채를 내며 훨훨 날갯짓해요

당신께 책 한 권 드려요

하얀 나비처럼 깨끗하고 자유로운 생애도 함께 드려요

Over yonder, I see a white butterfly flying away

I catch her with my white-gloved hand

Huu Huu

I place her carefully in a book

As she flaps, white sparkles from her wings fall on the pages of the book

Here is the book for you

I give you a free and spotless life, just like the white butterfly.

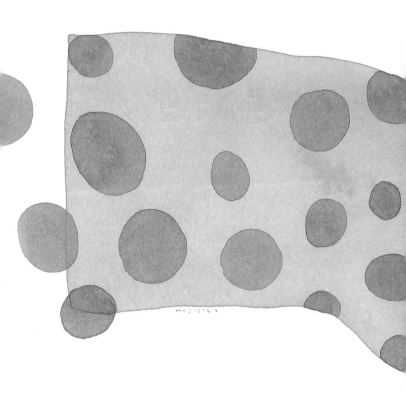

당신이 말했지

한 방울의 피가 빠져나가면 이제 마지막이야

한숨을 쉬며 대답했어

결국 여기까지 왔네요

하지만 모든 시간을 바쳐 간신히 모은 거잖아

양손을 모아 당신에게 바쳤고

손바닥이 갈라지며 한 송이 장미꽃이 피어났어

You told me

"Once a drop of blood escapes, that will be the end."

I answered you, heaving a sigh

"In the end, we end up coming this far.

It's been tough. I devoted all my time to gathering these drops.

I collected them all in my two hands and consecrated them to you

and as my palms cracked open, a stem of a rose bloomed forth.

There is a village which love has abandoned

The empty houses are full of crawling insects

Suddenly, the old broom, locked away in the cupboard so long ago,

appears in my mind

Soon after, the empty house has become clean, as have I

You have come back to my languid dream

It was my fault that love left in the first place.

사랑이 떠난 마을이 있어요

빈집마다 벌레들이 기어 다녀요

문득 오래전 창고에 넣어 두었던

빗자루가 떠올랐어요

잠시 후 빈집은 깨끗해졌고 저도 깨끗해졌어요

살포시 잠든 꿈속으로 당신이 돌아오셨네요

사랑이 떠나셨던 건 제 탓이군요

I pulled a crumpled white cloth from my mouth

by sticking a finger down my throat

After ironing the cloth with a scalding hot palm-iron

a white flag is now ready

I hang the white flag–a flag with no nationality-amid the flags of all nations

I placed myself up there as well

I see you running to me over the horizon.

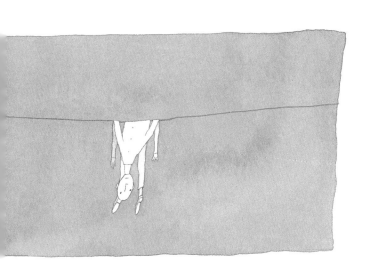

목구멍에 손가락을 넣어

구겨진 흰 천을 끄집어냈어

펄펄 끓는 손바닥 다리미로

하얀 깃발을 완성했지

알록달록 만국기 사이에 국적 없는 백기 하나 걸어놓았어

나도 거기 걸어두었어

멀리 지평선 너머를 달려오는 당신이 보여

알에서 깨어난 어린 새

the newly hatched bird

"This is live news, a newly hatched bird has started to fly in the sky"

"Mic testing"

"This is live news from the sky, called 'My dear love'"

"The newly born bird who has just learnt how to flap her little wings, is setting off fearlessly on a long journey"

"This was from the live scene, full of fuss and feathers."

알에서 깨어난 어린 새가 하늘을 날게 된 것을 알려드립니다

마이크 시험 중

이곳은 당신이라는 창공입니다

방금 날갯짓을 시작한 작은 새가 겁도 없이

긴 여정을 시작한 것을 알려드립니다

축제 분위기로 가득한 이곳 현장에서 전해드렸습니다

I spread my wings.

Flying in the sky is an amazing thing

Furr

I soared high up in the sky.

Why do I fly all alone?

Tears are about to fall

Furr

I become a bird.

I become the sky.

I see you waving from far away.

Your love put these wings on me.

I will return at the speed of light.

날개를 펼쳤어
하늘을 난다는 건 멋진 일이야
부웅
창공으로 날아올랐어
눈물이 떨어질 것 같아
혼자 날아야 하다니
비웅
새가 되었어
하늘이 되었어
멀리 손 흔드시는 당신이 보여
당신의 사랑이 날개를 달아주셨어요
빛의 속도로 돌아올게요

When I was a little girl, I learnt what life was all about on my granny's lap

As Granny stroked my forehead,

she used to say that life is all about joy and being proud

One day, everything seemed to change

But I know nothing has really changed

This morning, I learn about love by thinking of my Granny.

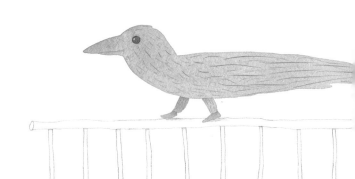

어릴 적 할머니 무릎에 앉아 인생을 배웠어요
이마를 쓰다듬어 주시며 할머니는 말하셨죠
기쁘고 자랑스러운 것이 인생이란다
어느 날 모든 게 변했어요
하지만 전 알아요 아무것도 달라진 게 없음을
오늘 아침 할머니를 떠올리며 사랑을 배워요

Have you ever seen a silently bowed bud suddenly bloom?

The flower calls out desperately, coloring her shy face red

"Am I doing all right?" she asks

Even in a time of turbulence and shameless bragging, she was still shy

I want to bloom alone in front of you, like her.

말없이 고개 숙인 꽃봉오리가 느닷없이 피어나는 걸 보셨나요
수줍은 얼굴을 빨갛게 물들이며 죽을 힘을 다해 외치더군요
저 잘하고 있나요
자랑질이 부끄럽지 않은 난세에도 꽃은 여전히 부끄러웠어요
호올로 당신 앞에서 꽃피고 싶어요

늙은 구렁이

an old python

If we want to tie today's love to tomorrow's,

we have to cross an uncharted river in our dreams

There may lurk an old python

which was transformed by the hatred in the air

But don't worry

Love, like a young carp, gleaming in the dream,

will guide us.

오늘 사랑이 내일 사랑으로 무사히 이어지려면
잠 속의 낯선 강물을 건너야 해요
대기 중에 가득한 증오가 늙은 구렁이로 변하여
물속에 숨어 있을 지도 모른다구요
걱정하지 마세요
꿈속에 어른거리는 젊은 잉어 같은 사랑이
우리를 인도할 거예요

I got lost

I wandered around and fell asleep in the street

A loathsome python slithered up to me and wound around my body

I killed him, wailing

I set off on my journey again

I fell asleep under a tree

Bracing wind patted my body

I hugged the breeze, laughing

It was you.

길을 잃었어요

헤매다가 길가에서 잠들었어요

징그러운 구렁이가 나타니 몸을 감았어요

울부짖으며 구렁이를 죽였어요

다시 길을 떠났어요

걷다가 나무 밑에서 잠들었어요

상쾌한 바람이 불어와 몸을 어루만졌어요

웃으며 바람을 껴안았어요

당신이셨어요

Once, I caught a huge fish

Somehow, it felt good

The fish said to me

"I am begging you, please let me go."

As the fish splashed back into the river

he turned into a python

The python turned back and said to me

"It wasn't easy letting you go, somehow,

 it felt good, I must have loved you."

큰 물고기를 잡았어

어쩐지 느낌이 좋았어

물고기가 말했어

부탁이에요 서를 놓아주세요

풍덩 강물에 들어간 물고기는

큼직한 구렁이로 변하더라구

뒤돌아보며 구렁이가 말했어

너를 놓아주는 게 쉽지는 않았어

어쩐지 느낌이 좋았어 널 사랑했나 봐

벌레로 변했어요

I turned into an insect

I hear the sounds of insects everywhere as I wake up in the morning

In the midst of a sleepless night, thinking of you, I turned into an insect

I was breath-taken by how many insects there were in the universe

There were more small ones than big ones

I felt the same deep pain they suffer

I was so sick because of love.

아침에 눈뜨니 사방에서 벌레 소리가 들렸어요
당신 생각에 잠 못 이루다 벌레로 변했어요
우주에는 정말 많은 벌레가 있더라구요
큰 것보다 작은 것이 훨씬 많더라구요
벌레들이 얼마나 아파하는지 덩달아 아팠어요
사랑 때문에 많이 아팠어요

Are you the light which dances in the sun or on the water?

You have touched me with sunlight and stroked me with glistening water

And now, even if I have to run with tears streaming down my face

I can't help but jump into your arms

into the dazzling sunlight, into the breathless and glimmering water,

into the big teardrop again.

당신은 햇살이신가요 물살이신가요

햇살로 어루만져 주시고 물살로 쓸어내려 주시면

저는 그저 눈물로 방울방울 뛰어다녀야 하지만

그래도 당신 품으로 뛰어들 수밖에 없네요

부신 햇살 속으로 숨찬 물살 속으로

다시 커다란 눈물 속으로

Once I met a monster with giant feet

Although I wanted to run to you, I couldn't

All I could do was look down at my growing feet

If there is a fairytale world where everything is so alluring, except me

I would love to live there for ever and ever

even though the forlorn spell would never be broken.

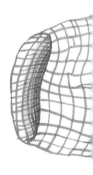

큰 발을 가진 괴물을 만난 적이 있어요

당신께 뛰어가 안기고 싶지만

커지는 발만 내려다본 적이 있거든요

나만 빼고 모든 것이 아름다운 동화 속 세상이 있다면

슬픈 마법이 풀리지 않아도 좋으니

거기서 영원히 살고 싶어요

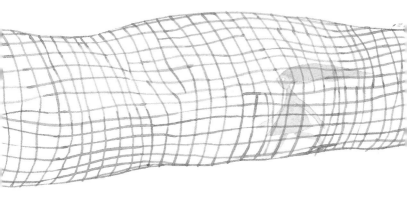

The water entered my body

The higher it got, the more out of breath I became

My whole body turned into water

A completely different world

Isn't it strange?

In the world of water, the one who hates

and the one who loves are not two but one

Sadly, the only thing the Goddess of Water permits is love.

물이 몸속으로 들어왔어요

물이 차오르다가 숨도 차올라요

몸이 온통 물로 변했어요

다른 세상이더군요

이상하죠

물의 나라에서는 미워하는 사람과

사랑하는 사람이 둘이 아니라 하나더군요

물이 허락하는 것은 슬프게도 오직 사랑뿐이더군요

슬픔이 파도처럼 밀려왔어

파도는 나를 덥석 안아 올리더니 무등을 태워주었지

파도의 손끝에서 환호하던 나는

이제 머얼리 포구를 빠져나가는 중이야

알아요 밀어닥친 파도가 당신이었다는 걸

혼비백산 솟구친 슬픔의 클라이맥스도

당신이었다는 걸

Sadness surged up like waves

The waves suddenly grasped me and took me for a ride

Rejoicing on the tip of the waves

-I know I am on my way out of this harbour

I know the sweeping waves were you

I also know that the climax of my thunder stricken,

bursting sorrow was you too.

삐이걱 펌프질 소리가 들리던 외갓집의 마당

키 작은 봉숭아 같던 외할머니

갓 태어난 송아지 같던 나

시간의 유리벽을 뚫고

그리로 가려면

잊혀야 할 순간이 너무 많아

봉숭아꽃 물들이던 그 가을로 날아가려면

버려야 할 서러움이 너무 많아

Granny's front garden where I used to hear the creaking sound of water pumping

My granny who was so much like a tiny garden balsam

Myself - so much like a new born calf

To return there

to slide through the glass wall of time

there are an awful lot of moments to be forgotten

To fly back to that autumn of balsam-dyed finger nails

there are an awful lot of sorrows that need to evaporate.

이미 늦은 것 같아

그걸 되찾으려면 쓰레기 더미를 뒤적여야 하는데

오래 전 사랑의 낙서 촌닭 같은 애정의 고백

아지랑이 봄날로 가기엔 벌써 늦은 것 같아

손에 쥔 쪽지 하나 펴보지도 못했는데

가을날 찬비에 젖어버렸네

널 잊지 않을 거야

Perhaps it's way too late

I will have to dumpster dive to get it back

but the scribblings on love I wrote from so long ago, these confessions of love –

so like a callow chicken, they are too late to go to the soft haze of a spring day

The scrap of paper I clasped in my hand hasn't even been unfolded

It still got soaking wet in the cold rain of that Autumn day

I will never forget you.

물속에서 눈을 감아요

몸서리치는 냉기가 느껴져요

눈물이 몸에서 빠져나가요

저기 반짝이는 건 당신의 눈물인가요

사박사박 저리로 가요

하얀 면사포를 쓰리니 눈물의 다이아몬드를 끼워주세요

우리 사랑을 약속하면 추운 세상이 따스해질까요

I close my eyes under the water

I feel the shivering chill

Tears are escaping from my body

Is that sparkling your tear?

I take light steps towards you

Please, put that diamond-like tear on me as I put on my white wedding veil

Would this frosty world turn warm the moment we exchange vows to our love?

물 한 바가지

a bowl of water

There is a moment

when we are lost in a desert

when the road seems endless, regardless of how far we've gone.

A moment when we want to drop down and sob;

a moment when even our tears dry up and makes us feel so blocked up.

A moment when I miss you holding a bowl of water,

when I see you offering me a glass of water

when tears well up in my eyes

when I fall into your arms.

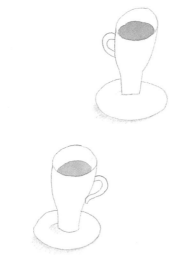

그럴 때가 있잖아

사막에서 길을 잃을 때

가도 가도 끝이 없을 때

주저앉아 울고 싶을 때

답답하게 눈물마저 마를 때

물동이 들고 계신 당신이 그리울 때

물 한 바가지 건네시는 당신이 보일 때

핑그르 눈물이 돌 때

당신 품에 안길 때

I walked in the rain

Tears dropped like rain

Suddenly, I wanted to feel the rain without a brolly

Cos' I felt like the rain was going to wash away my tears

Just as a brolly was suddenly thrown away,

magically, the rain stopped

The crystalline sunshine wiped away my tears

The dear Sun–so much like you–even handed me a soft, fluffy towel.

빗속을 걸었어

빗물처럼 눈물도 흘렀어

문득 우산 없이 비를 맞고 싶어졌어

빗물이 눈물마저 씻어줄 것 같았거든

멀찍이 우산을 던지는 순간

거짓말처럼 비가 그쳤어

말간 햇살이 눈물을 닦아주었어

당신을 닮은 해님이 뽀송한 수건까지 건네주셨어

고추잠자리 따라 하늘로 올라가요

빙글 하늘 속으로 들어가요

노란 국화가 손짓해요

돌아와, 조금 더 가면 돌아올 수 없을 거야

고추잠자리를 하늘로 놓아 보내고 풀 죽어 당신 품으로 파고들어요

말없이 토닥여 주는 손길에

가만히 눈을 감아요

Following a red dragonfly, I am heading up to the sky

I am swirling in the sky

The yellow chrysanthemum beckons

"Come back! If you go any further, you won't be able to return."

I let go of the red dragonfly and flop into your arms, snuggling

As you pat me in silence

I gently close my eyes.

돌을 던졌어

퐁당퐁당 당신 가슴속으로 던졌어

슬그머니 나도 따라 들어갔어

숨죽이며 사방을 둘러보았어

쓸쓸하더군

치맛귀 살짝 올리며 퐁당퐁당 춤을 추었어

사방이 환해졌어

돌아나오며 뒤를 돌아보았지

산속 오두막에 등불 하나 켜져 있더군

I threw a stone

plop plop into your heart

I sneakily went into your heart with the stone

I looked around, holding my breath.

It was desolate.

Lifting the tip of my skirt, I started dancing; plop, plop.

Everything started to lighten up.

I looked back as I was leaving.

I saw a single light on, in a cottage in the forest.

A sharp gut-wrenching pain stabbed my tummy

I rubbed around it with my eyes closed

Vague memories returned; of me aboard a boat

The people who had loved but failed to fulfil their love

got on the boat and rowed out, following their memories

I met a beautiful person on this water journey.

I shared a dream-like love with him.

배가 아팠어 날카로운 통증이 배를 찔렀어

눈 감고 배를 어루만졌어

아련한 기억이 배를 타고 왔어

사랑하였으나 사랑을 완성하지 못한 사람들

배 위에 올라타고 기억 따라 노를 저었어

아름다운 사람을 물길에서 만났어

꿈결 같은 사랑을 나누었어

딸기코

a warm feeling

혼자라는 생각이 들어 문득 서러웠어요

어쩌면 당신조차 잠시 잊었나 봐요

따뜻한 느낌이 코끝을 찡하게 하더군요

점점 코가 부풀어 딸기코가 되었어요

푸핫 웃음이 터지며 당신이 떠올라요

혼자가 아니라는 생각이 들어 참 다행이에요

All of a sudden, I am in sorrow as I sense the loneliness

I may have even forgotten about you for a bit

A warm feeling flares up on the tip of my nose

My nose becomes all swollen and red – like a strawberry

As I hoot with laughter, you come in to my mind

I am glad to know that I am not alone.

당신과 저는 하나의 담에

나란히 기댄 두 집과 같아요

문득 서러운 생각이 드네요

우리 사이에 담벼락이라니요

조용히 웃으시는 당신 얼굴이 보여요

존재의 경계를 녹여주시는 당신의 미소가

한량없는 축복이라는 걸 알아요

You and I are like two semi-detached houses,

leaning onto one wall but separated

I am woeful all of a sudden

"Why on earth do we have a wall between us?"

I see your face, smiling peacefully

It is the tender smile melting the borders of two separate existences

I understand that your smile is an immeasurable blessing.

술래잡기를 했어

내가 술래였고 찾아야 할 사람은 당신이었지

눈에는 하얀 수건이 둘러 있었어

왜 그리 눈물이 흐르던지 영원이 흐른 것 같았어

수건이 바닥에 떨어졌고

당신이 웃고 있더군

무얼 찾는 거야

나 언제나 여기 당신 곁에 있었는데

I played hide-and-seek

I was to seek and you were to be hidden

My eyes were covered by a white cloth

The rivers of tears were running down as if they were running for eternity

The white cloth fell from my eyes

And I saw you smiling at me

"What have you been searching for?"

"I have always been with you, right here."

고사리손을 꼭 쥐며 아빠를 올려다보았어

느닷없이 빈손을 놓았고

평생 아빠 찾아 삼만리를 포기하지 않았어

놀랍게도 당신은 곁에 계셨던 거야

갈퀴손을 꽉 쥐며

아빠를 내려다볼 생각을 이제야 하다니

사랑 열차도 왕복을 끊어야 했던 거야

I looked up to see my daddy with my little tighten fern hand

Out of the blue, I let go of that empty hand

I had never given up searching for my daddy, no matter how far I had to go

To my surprise, Dad, you have always been here, beside me

How daft of me to take this long to look down at my daddy

with my tightly clenched hand

I now know we need to buy return tickets for the coach of love.

오뚝이를 처음 본 순간 사랑에 빠졌어
신나는 오뚝이 춤을 손뼉 치며 바라보았지
다시 오뚝이를 만난 건 녹아웃 직전이었어
어느새 사각의 링에 갇혀 있었던 거야
당신 손을 잡고 일어나 황홀한 듀엣을 추었지
그렇게 링 밖으로 걸어 나왔던 거야

When I first saw the *Ottogi*, I fell in love with it at first sight

I remember my hands clapping while watching the cheerful *Ottogi* dancing.

When next I saw the *Ottogi*, before I knew it,

I found myself trapped in a boxing ring, about to be knocked out

I got up by holding your hand and danced an entrance duet

That is how I escaped the ring.

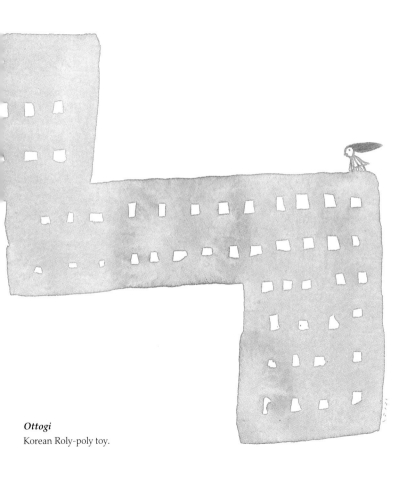

Ottogi
Korean Roly-poly toy.

I saw a swimming carp in a pond

It's you hidden behind the lotus leaf but it is so vivid before me

When the dazzling red carp jumps, the bottle-green lotus leaf leaps too

I remember the story of a pond world

They say the carp will turn into a dragon one day

Just like that ending, I know that our life will be completed with love.

연못을 헤엄치는 잉어를 보았어요

연잎에 가린 당신이지만 눈앞에 선연해요

선홍빛 잉어가 뛰어오르면 진녹색 연잎도 피어올라요

연못 나라의 이야기가 기억나요

잉어는 마침내 용이 된다네요

우리의 생애도 그렇게 사랑으로 완성될 것을 믿어요

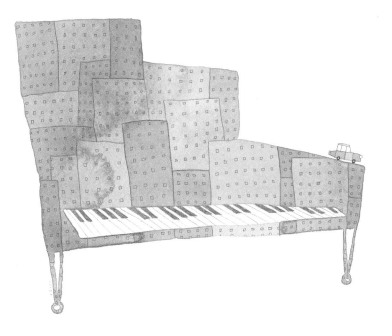

딸기코

a warm feeling

7-7

아침마다 눈뜨면 아기처럼 태어나요

두리번 세상을 보고

아리송 세상이 궁금해요

아장아장 걸어가니

산이 보이고 새가 들려요

그리고 나무 뒤에 당신이 서 있네요

까르르 숨바꼭질 놀이에 해가 기울어요

저녁마다 눈 감으면

아기처럼 잠들어요

When I wake up every morning, I become a new-born baby

I look around in wonder

then I get curious about this cryptic world

Toddle waddle I walk

I see mountains and hear birds tweeting

There you are, standing behind the tree

The Sun goes down amid the peals of laughter of hide-and-seek

When I close my eyes every evening,

I drift away, like a new-born baby.

깊은 산속 옹달샘

a small spring in a deep forest

I know a small spring in a deep forest

It's in your mind

Lost and all alone, I found a spring and took a mouthful of water

I am not going to get lost again

If I lose my way and stumble, I will run back there

Please give me a mouthful of love

If you do, I will remember my way instantly.

깊은 산속 옹달샘을 알아요

당신 마음속에 있어요

홀로 길 잃어 발견했다가 물 한 모금 받아 마시고 왔어요

다시 길 잃지 않을 거예요

길 몰라 비틀거리면 그곳으로 달려갈래요

사랑 한 모금 주세요

잃어버린 길이 퍼뜩 떠오를 거예요

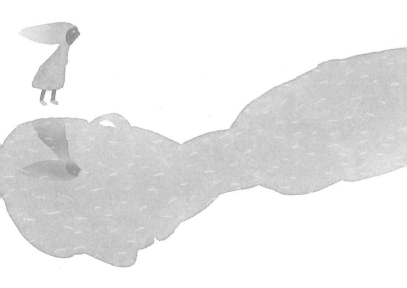

The sky is in you

I can see the blue sky, pregnant with white cumulus clouds, floating

Nobody has been there, not even you

Only I have been there

I would love to take you there.

하늘이 그대 안에 있다

새하얀 뭉게구름 두둥실 뜬 새파란 하늘이 보인다

아무도 그곳에 가본 적 없다 당신조차 그런 것 같다

오직 나만 그곳에 다녀왔다

당신을 모시고 그곳에 가고 싶다

I hear a loud pounding sound

I am not sure even if it is a sound

I throw myself into the sound of non-sound

It's inside your heart

How stunning!

It is a new world, full of happiness with not a single sorrow

It is a world that only becomes real through your love.

큰 소리가 들려요 쿵쿵거리는 소리예요

소리가 아닌지도 모르겠어요

소리 아닌 소리 속으로 몸을 던져요

당신 가슴속이군요

놀라워요

슬픔 없는 세상 행복으로만 가득찬 세상 새로운 세상이군요

당신의 사랑 속에서 비로소 현실이 되는 세상이군요

When I look at you, I remember the kaleidoscope

I used to keep in a drawer when I was a little girl

As the tiny little pieces of paper present rhapsodic images,

your trivial gestures present quivering spectacular scenes

I say loud and clear to my late father

"Daddy, I got it back!"

당신을 보고 있으니 어린 시절 서랍 속에 간직하던
만화경이 떠올라요
작은 종이 조각들이 황홀한 광경을 연출하듯이
사소한 당신의 몸짓들이 설레는 장관을 펼치네요
돌아가신 아버지에게 큰 소리로 말해요
아빠 그거 다시 찾았어요

'Cos I could see you in the glorious silvery moon

I scaled a ladder, up into the sky, and brought the full moon back in my arms

The full moon came straight into my rounded arms while I was dreaming of you

I could see the sky had become as black as the River Styx

I climbed back up, and hung the full moon there, up in the sky

I left myself there, too…

사다리 걸고 하늘에 올라 보름달을 안아왔어

휘영청 그곳에 당신이 보였거든

당신을 꿈꾸다 둥글어진 품으로 보름달이 들어왔어

보름달을 껴안다 캄캄해진 하늘이 보였어

다시 하늘에 올라 보름달을 걸고 왔어

나도 따라 그곳에 두고 왔어

I have just returned from the far end of the universe

The end had always been a pitch black cliff

but this end was a splendid gleaming field

It was a fluttering, not a fear

I have opened a new mill inside of my body

with the bag of rice you gave me

I know now that I have just returned

from my very first trip around the village.

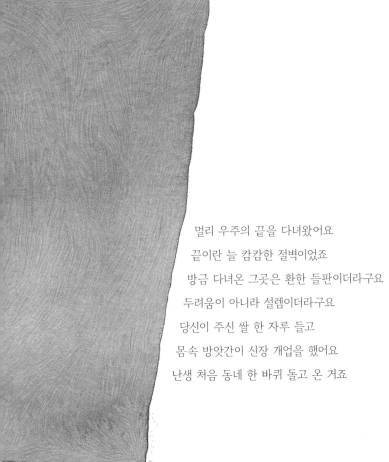

멀리 우주의 끝을 다녀왔어요

끝이란 늘 캄캄한 절벽이었죠

방금 다녀온 그곳은 환한 들판이더라구요

두려움이 아니라 설렘이더라구요

당신이 주신 쌀 한 자루 들고

몸속 방앗간이 신장 개업을 했어요

난생 처음 동네 한 바퀴 돌고 온 거죠

어젯밤 꿈에 말야

작은 안경을 코에 걸고

멀리 세상을 돌아다녔어

한동안 앞이 보이지 않았거든 땅속 두더지처럼 눈이 멀어갔거든

아름다운 풍경이었어

갑자기 찌푸린 하늘이 맑게 개더라구

풍경 속에 그림처럼 웃고 계신 당신 모습이 보였거든

In my dream last night

I travelled far across the world with a pair of small specks sliding down my nose

I haven't been able to see a thing for quite a while

because my eyesight has gotten weaker, just like a mole underground

I saw breathtaking scenery

When I spotted you smiling amidst the scenery, like a painting

the frowning sky brightened up, just like that.

아침이 왔어요

morning has come

Morning has come

How can I be so sure?

Some people are telling me that it could still be night

But I know it's morning because you woke me up

because you gave my heart pins and needles with your touch

How am I so sure that it was your touch?

It's obvious because it is only you

who can make me weep for happiness.

아침이 왔어요

어떻게 확신하냐구요

아직도 밤일지 모른다구요

당신이 저를 깨우셨거든요

뭉클하는 손길로 가슴을 저리게 하셨거든요

당신의 손인지 어떻게 확신하냐구요

틀림없어요 제게 행복한 눈물을 짓게 하는 건

당신밖에 없으니까요

남루한 아침을 열며 눈물을 뿌렸지요

줄 것이 없는 빈 깡통 같은 사랑이 부끄러웠어요

고개 숙이고 돌아눕는데 흰 머리카락이 눈앞을 막아서요

손들어 가리려다가 당신의 어색한 미소가 떠올랐어요

받기만 한 보물섬 같은 사랑이 기뻐요

사랑해요

As I opened a shabby morning, I sprinkled my tears down

Embarrassed with my empty-canned love – nothing to give

As I lower my head and roll onto one side, a strand of grey covers my face

As I lift my hand to hide the grey in shame, your awkward smile appears

The love I have only received but never given back, like a treasure island,

is marvellous. I love you.

당신이 주신 선물이 나를 얼마나

행복하게 했는지 모르실 거예요

그게 뭐냐구요

잘 모르겠어요

정말 받기는 했냐구요

세상에서 가장 값진 선물을 받았죠

대체 뭐냐구요

모르겠어요

그 선물이 나를 행복하게 했다는 것 말고

아무것도 모르겠다구요

You haven't got the slightest idea how much happiness

you brought me with your gift

Are you asking me what it was?

I don't know

Are you asking me if I have indeed received it?

Yes, I have - the most invaluable of gifts from you

Are you asking me what that is then?

I am not so sure

The only thing I know is whatever you gave me

has raised me up to happiness.

A tiny old lady said,

"Eons, eons ago, a giant of a man loved me."

She was dragged into her dreamy eyes and has never returned

I cottoned on to what the old lady had in mind

Love wasn't meant to be in the arms of a giant

but in a little kid's bare fists.

조그만 할머니가 말했어
옛날 옛적 간날 간적에 큰큰 할아버지가
나를 사랑하셨지
꿈꾸는 눈동자 속으로 들어가버린 할머니는
더 이상 나오지 않았지만
나는 할머니의 마음을 알아버렸어
사랑은 거인의 품속이 아니라
꼬마의 맨주먹 속에 있는 거였어

My heart pounded when I first saw your smile

It started to beat

then it became mushy, crumpled up and collapsed

It fell down to the floor boards, then dropped down under the floor

I hunkered down there

and recalled your smile over and over and over

There are precious things under the old floor

It is the place where I head for when I am saddened.

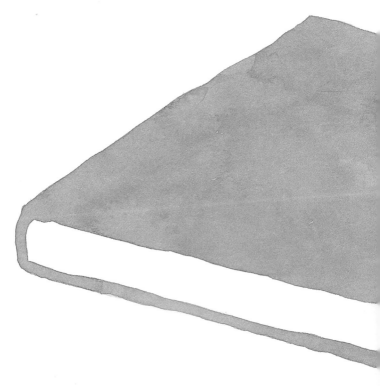

당신의 미소를 처음 보았을 때 내 가슴은 뛰었어요

뛰다가 흐물흐물 무너졌어요

끼익 마룻장이 무너지면서

마루 밑으로 떨어졌어요

쪼그리고 앉아

당신의 미소를 자꾸만 떠올려요

오래된 마루 밑에는 소중한 것들이 있어요

슬플 때면 그리로 가요

꿀벌이 꿀을 모으는 걸 봤어

위잉위잉 낮게 날았어

뜨거운 대지에서 혼신의 힘으로 몰두하고 있었어

꽃들이 꿀을 허락하는 걸 볼 수 있게 된 건

한참의 세월이 흐른 후였어

윙윙 꿀벌 소리에 가려

꽃들의 아름다운 침묵이 들리지 않았던 거야

I saw a bee sucking out the nectar

buzzing low–buzz, buzz

They were engrossed with all their heart and soul on the scorching earth

I started to sense much later that it was the flowers allowing

the bees to take the nectar

I couldn't hear it because the flowers' stunning silence

was concealed beneath the bees' buzzing.

당신의 사랑에는 뭐든지 들어 있어

사르르 별사탕도 있고

화르르 성냥갑도 있어

보들보들 강아지 젤리도 있고

에헴 할아버지 인형도 있어

종합선물세트 같은 당신 주머니 안에

나도 들어갈래

주머니 속 선물이 되어

어느 빈손에 전해지면 좋겠어

Your love holds everything imaginable,

literally everything

Soft-melting starry sweets,

flare-busting match boxes,

silky-smooth puppy jelly,

Ahem! A grandpa doll - just like an assorted gift set.

I want to join them inside your pocket

I would be delighted if I can be one of your gifts

and be passed into an empty hand sometime.

단 한 번의 입맞춤

one single kiss

I dare to complete love with one single kiss

If I can taste love, just once, taste the subtlety of its sweet yet bitter,

elegant yet vulgar

I would be happy to take it as the end

Let's write a legendary story on our lips

The story of ending one's life with a one-off love

even a single drop of saliva will be saccharine as honey.

단 한 번의 입맞춤으로 사랑을 완성하고 싶어

달콤하고 쓸쓸하고 우아하고 천박한 묘미를

단번에 맛볼 수 있다면

여기서 끝나도 좋아

한 번의 사랑으로 생애를 마감하는 전설 같은 이야기를

우리 입술 위에 써요

한 방울의 침도 꿀처럼 달콤할 거야

"Please dawn, come slower for me tonight,

even if it means that I and my darling will freeze to death

after making love on this bamboo leaf bed,

laid as it is, on an icy floor."

– tribute to ManJeonChoon

You too, are buried and ossified under the ground

Oh, how I so miss the love that you both shared

in this world where nothing becomes hot

unless one becomes a tiger moth and hovers around the seductive flame.

Man-Jeon-Choon

Man-Jeon-Choon is a pop song from *Goryeo*, a Korean dynasty lasting from AD. 918 to 1392. The writer of the song is unknown. *Man-Jeon-Choon* was banned by the scholar-officials during the Joseon dynasty (1392 -1910) as it was deemed to be lewd. With an emotive use of language, *Man-Jeon-Choon* speaks frankly about human love within the context of nature.

어름 우희 댓닙 자리 보와

님과 나와 어러주글만뎡

정둔 오날밤 더듸 새오시라

백골 되어 땅 밑에 누운 당신들의 사랑이 그립구나

부나방 되어 카바이트 불 옆을 서성이지 않으면

더 이상 뜨거워지지 않는 세상에서

-tribute to 만전춘

만전춘(滿殿春)
고려 시대(AD.918–1392)에 지어진 작자 미상의 속요. 속요란 대중가요의 노랫말.
조선 시대의 사대부 즉 규범적 지식인에 의해 음탕한 노래로 규정되어 배척되었다.
자연 속에서 이루어지는 인간의 진솔한 삶과 사랑이 감성적인 언어로 아름답게 표현되었다.

길 잃은 짐승처럼 울부짖고 다녔어

벌판을 지나 인가로 들어섰어

인간의 자취는 묘연한데 짐승의 자취가 느껴졌어

킁킁 따라가 보니 당신이 서 계셨어

이상하지 어디에도 없던 인간의 냄새 짐승 같은 당신 품에서 그걸 느끼다니

막다른 길에서였어

I wandered around, howling like a lost beast

I passed the fields and approached a house

I couldn't see any signs of people but sensed the scent of an animal

I sniffed the air and found you standing right before me

How strange that I felt a human scent from a beastly you, in your arms?

It was a dead end after all.

사랑이 모든 것의 시작이에요

광장의 단상에서 외치는 별 같은 분도

사랑을 전할 수 없다면

빈 수레 되어 구석에 처박힐 거예요

골목의 상자에서 꼼틀대는 길냥이도

사랑을 얻을 수 있다면

언젠가 하늘의 별이 될 거예요

사랑이 모든 것의 끝이에요

Love is the start of everything

Even someone who is at the height of their stardom now will end up alone

and forgotten if they can't convey what love is

Even a lowly street cat

squirming in an old abandoned box down in the gutter

can one day arise like a star in the night sky

if she is loved

Love is the end of everything.

I stab your heart with the end of a needle

One single drop should be the right dose of love

It must be just the right amount

Life must be the same

But to make it work

I shall become a naked baby, just like Cupid.

To move in and out of you.

To get into every single corner of you.

For that, you will have to give me access to your heart.

바늘 끝으로 당신의 심장을 찔러요
한 방울이 사랑의 정량이겠지요
딱 그만큼이겠지요
인생도 그렇겠지요
하지만 그게 가능하려면요
큐피트처럼 벌거숭이 아이 되어
속속들이 당신 속을
드나들어야 하잖아요
제게 당신의 심장을 허락해주셔야 하잖아요

다시 태어난다면 작은 서랍이 되고 싶어

당신의 마음을 조용히 품고 있으면 다시 열리지 않아도 괜찮을 거야

우연히 날아든 나비 장신구를 소중히 간직하고 있다가

당신의 어딘가에서 단 한 번 반짝일 수 있다면

더 이상 태어나지 않아도 좋을 거야

If I am ever reborn, I fancy being a tiny drawer

I will be fine being locked up forever as long as I embrace you in silence

I will be fine even though I never have another life

as long as I can sparkle for one split second in you somewhere

with a butterfly ornament, which I have held in keeping, so preciously for you.

아침마다 눈뜨면 세상 끝으로 달려가

모래성을 지어요

어느새 세상 속으로 돌아와

눈 흘김 주고받으며 살아가지만

그곳에 계신 당신을 잊을 수 있나요

세상에서 제일 견고한 당신의 모래성이 없다면

슬픈 세월 잠시도 견딜 수 없을 거예요

Every morning when I wake up, I run to the end of the world

to build a sandcastle

Before I know it, I am back in the real world,

living under the exchange of glares and stares

but how can I forget you, living there?

Without the stoutest sandcastle of you,

I won't be able to bear these mournful days for even a split second.

우리의 인연

our Nidana

"Will our Nidana be connected again somewhere

after a thousand years has passed?"

No, probably not

The reason why our love is so splendid is because it is like a fleeting bubble

Perhaps that's why I tend to avoid such thoughts

No!

That's not true!

I will love you forever.

다시 천 년의 시간이 흐르면

우리의 인연은 어디에서 이어질까요

그렇지 않아요

우리 사랑이 눈부신 까닭은 찰나의 물거품이기 때문일 거예요

차마 삼가는 마음도 그래서 생겨났을 거예요

아니에요

그렇지 않아요

당신을 영원히 사랑할 거예요

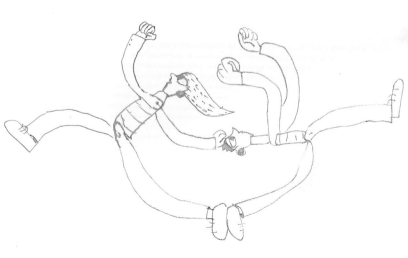

산신령 할아버지

국토의 70퍼센트가 산이며 야트막하고
친근한 산이 많은 한국에는 예로부터
산신 신앙이 전해온다. 산신은 하얀
수염을 늘어뜨린 할아버지의 모습을
하고 있으며, 호랑이를 거느리고
지팡이를 짚고 있다. 착한 아이처럼
자연에 기대어 살아가는 인간의 소원을
들어주는 자애로운 자연의 영혼이
있다고 믿는 소박한 기대를 의인화한
것이 '산신령 할아버지'이다.

San-Shil-Yeong Hal-Ah-Beo-Jee; The guardian spirit of a mountain

Mountains cover 70 percent of
Korea. In Korea, with her numerous
low range hills and intimate
mountains, has seen the mountain
spirit being passed down through
generations. The mountain spirit is
said to have a lolling white beard,
and is depicted with a wooden
walking stick and accompanied by a
tiger. The austere hope of believing
in the existence of a benevolent spirit
of nature which grants human's
wishes – leaves people living their
lives depending on nature like docile
children. *San-Shil-Yeong Hal-Ah-Beo-Jee* is the anthropomorphised norms
of such austere hope.

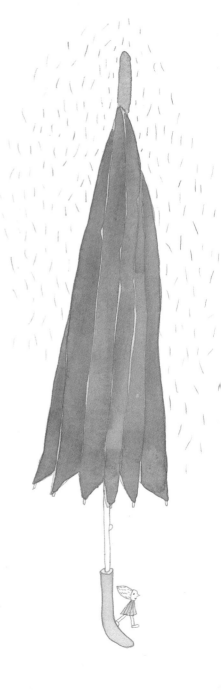

비가 오시네요

저도 모르게 빗속으로 걸어갔어요

당신의 사랑에 흠뻑 젖어 한세상 지나고 싶어요

우산도 비옷도 없이 인생을 맞이하게 하신 당신께 감사드려요

하얀 수염이 빗물에 흠뻑 젖은 산신령 할아버지가

당신 뒤에 서 계시네요

It's raining

Before I knew it, I found myself walking in the rain

I want to pass this life by being soaked wet with your love

Thank you for letting me have this life without an umbrella or a raincoat

An old, white bearded *San-Shil-Yeong Hal-Ah-Beo-Jee*, drenched wet by the rain,

is standing behind you.

I give you a cluster of cosmos flowers

I see you wreathed in smiles

I have now fulfilled the promise I made in the beginning

Thank God I made it

If it were not love, I could have easily forgotten this precious promise

that I would give you a million clusters of universes, all of them.

한 송이 코스모스를 당신께 드려요

환하게 웃는 당신 얼굴이 보이네요

태초의 약속을 이제야 지키게 되었어요

천만다행이에요

사랑이 아니었다면 귀한 약속 잊을 뻔 했으니까요

백만 송이 우주를 온통 당신께 드리겠다는 아름다운 약속 말이에요

I couldn't raise my head for a while

All I could see was people's feet

They were all wearing filthy shoes

I got embarrassed for reasons I can't explain

One day I saw a pair of pale, bare feet

I knew that I was going to fall in love with you without even looking up.

한동안 고개를 들 수 없었어

문득 사람들의 발이 보이더군

모두들 더러운 구두를 신고 있었어

공연히 부끄러웠지

어느 날 하얀 맨발이 보이더군

올려다 보지 않아도 모든 걸 알 수 있었어 당신을 사랑하게 될 거라는 걸

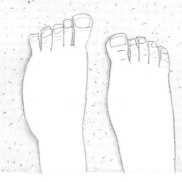

I walk the streets, covered by the blanket of a squalid life

As I turn down an alley, I see your back over there

I run to you in a rush

but all I find is clear starlight, swirling around

I soar upwards, letting out a wail

I honestly don't care if I have to spend my entire life flying to reach your star

Would it even matter if it took millions of light years?

누추한 삶을 뒤집어쓰고 길을 걸어요

골목길 돌아가는데 저만치 당신의 등이 보여요

와르르 뛰어가보니

맑은 별빛만 감돌아요

통곡하며 날아올라요

남은 생애 모두 써도 아깝지 않아요

당신의 별로 날아가는 데

몇 만 광년을 쓰면 어떻겠어요

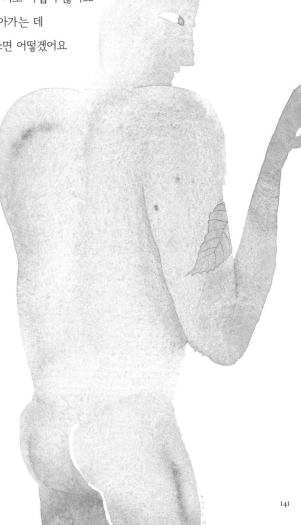

하늘에서 꽃비가 내려요

고개 들고 팔 벌려

꽃비를 맞아요

입안 가득 꽃 물고 당신을 꿈꾸어요

기적 같은 꽃비를 목놓아 기다린 건 당신 때문이에요

꽃을 사랑하다 꽃이 되어버린 오늘

보드란 꽃의 살결에 볼 부비며 당신을 기다려요

Flowery-rain is falling from the sky

With my head thrown back and outstretched arms

I welcome this flowery-rain

I dream of you with a mouth brimming with flowers

The only reason I so desperately crave this miraculous flowery-rain is you

Today, I turn into a flower, after having loved this flower for so long

I wait for you as I caress my cheek with a pearly petal.

고마워요

이렇게 옹색하게나마 세상에 마음 붙이고 살아가는 것도

모두 당신 때문인 걸요

그럼 사랑은요

어른스러운 고마움이 아이 같은 사랑을 지워버리면 어쩌냐구요

아니야

이 길이 맞아

이정표에 써 있어

고마운 당신을 죽을 만큼 사랑해

Thank you

It is all because of you that I can at least bear my life in this world

"What about love then?"

Are you asking me what if this childlike love is erased

by a matured appreciation

No

This is the right way

It's written on the signpost

I am grateful for you, and I love you enough to die for you

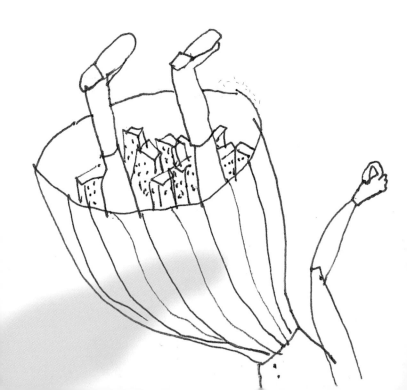

천사를 만난 적이 있나요

날개 달린 어린 천사는 아니지만

우연히 지나친 키 작은 할머니가 천사라고 믿었어요

당신을 미워한 적 없어요

눈 흘기거나 꼬집은 적도 없어요

당신이 저를 천사로 만드셨어요

작지만 착한 마음을 가진 당신의 천사가 될래요

Have you ever met an angel?

I once believed a tiny old lady I bumped into in the street was an angel –

not a youthful angel with a pair of wings

I have never hated you

Nor have I glared at you or even given you a pinch

You turned me into an angel

I want to be your little yet sweet-hearted angel.

Jeogori
Upper garment of Korean female traditional dress.

I have put on a snow-white *Jeogori* with a scarlet skirt, pinned a red butterfly

worn shyness with the wedding rouge on my cheeks and forehead

All done

You shall come before the Moon rises

I'll whinge in your arms

telling you that living this life wasn't easy

However, I am going to welcome in another life

a most splendid world holding your hand.

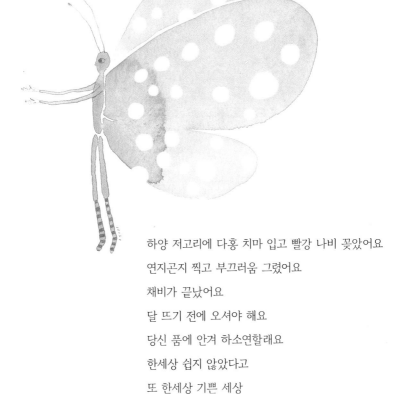

하양 저고리에 다홍 치마 입고 빨강 나비 꽂았어요

연지곤지 찍고 부끄러움 그렸어요

채비가 끝났어요

달 뜨기 전에 오셔야 해요

당신 품에 안겨 하소연할래요

한세상 쉽지 않았다고

또 한세상 기쁜 세상

당신 손 맞잡고 꼬옥 맞이하련다고

A pair of sparrows with rounded bellies and plump faces, flew in

chattering tattling – so much to talk about

Poruerue, they soar up

Soruerue, they fly down

Within the merest of moments in my trip through the clear autumn sunshine,

the sparrows had flown away

I quickly picked up a brush and drew the pair of birds into my heart.

참새 두 마리가 날아왔어

배는 볼록하고 얼굴은 통통해 재잘재잘 할 말은 왜 그리 많은지

포르르 날아올랐다

소르르 내려앉곤 해

맑은 가을 햇살 속으로 깜빡 다녀온 사이

참새가 날아갔어

수채 붓을 들어 가슴속에 두 마리를 얼른 그려 넣었어

작은 문

a small door

I am standing before a small door

I see a rusty keyhole

I know if I can just open this door

everything will become possible

As I recall your deep hug

I started to scream under my breath

as loud as the whole world can roar

"Please open this tiny door."

After a little while

the door opened magically.

작은 문 앞에 서 있어
녹슨 열쇠 구멍이 보여
작은 문을 열 수 있다면
모든 게 이루어질 것을 알아
당신의 가슴팍을 떠올리며
온 세상이 울릴 만큼
작은 소리로 외쳤어
세상에서 제일 작은 이 문을 열어주세요
잠시 후
기적처럼 문이 열렸어

고양이를 따라갔어

골목길을 지나 작은 문 앞에 섰어

고양이는 사라졌고 덜컥 문이 열렸어

문 뒤에 당신이 서 계셨지

왈칵 가슴이 무너졌어

문은 열린 게 아니라 열어주신 거구나

당신을 따라 새로운 세상으로 달려가며 외쳤어

고양이가 그랬어

I followed a cat

As I passed an alley, I stopped in front of a door

The cat disappeared and the door opened sharply

There you were, behind the door

My whole heart sank

The door didn't just open; you opened it

I started to shout with joy as I followed you into a new world

The cat was the author of all this.

마법 따위 믿지 않았어

아무것도 아닌 사랑에 빠졌을 뿐이야

홀연히 마법에 걸린 세상이 보였어

고운 물고기들이 진흙탕에서 울고 있었거든

슬그머니 손가락을 들어

사랑의 마법을 써보았어

아아

모든 것이 달라지더군

진짜 마법 같은 일이었어

I never used to believe in magic

It was just the simple act of falling in love

but from it I could instantly see an enchanted world

because I could see the pretty fish, sobbing in the mire

Lifting my finger stealthily

I had a go at the magic of love

Blimey!

Everything changed

It was so very magical.

하늘 향해 손가락 편지를 써요

너무 더워요

오곡백과 무르익는 가을은 언제 오는 건가요

한층 맑아진 입추의 하늘은 말이 없으시지만요

귀또리가 튀어나와 종알거려요 귀뚤귀뚤 귀또르르

말없이 두 손 모으니

황금빛 넘실대는 가을 들판이 보여요

I write a letter on to the sky with my finger

"It's way too hot."

"When will the Autumn

-the season of the five grains and hundred ripened fruits-arrive?"

Though your much clearer sky on *Ip-chu*

can't say a word

A cricket jumps out chirping; chirr chirr chirrrr

I see the brimful of golden Autumn fields appearing

as hands come together, without a word.

입추(立秋)

입추는 24절기의 13번째 절기이며, 가을이 시작되는
시점이다. 양력으로 8월 8일경. 쓰르라미가 울고,
서늘한 바람이 불기 시작하고, 이슬이 내린다.
24절기는 태양의 황도상 위치에 따라 계절을
구분하기 위해 만든 것으로, 농경 사회인 한국
전통 사회의 시간 개념을 지배했다.

Ip-Chu; **The Start of Autumn**

Ip-Chu is the 13th of the 24 seasons in the
traditional Korean calendar, referring to the
transition to Autumn. *Ip-Chu* is on the 8th of
August in the solar calendar. It is the time when
the crickets start to chirp, cool breezes arrive and
dew starts to fall. In the context of a traditionally
agricultural Korean society, these 24 seasons are
determined by the ecliptic position of the Sun
and are used to determine the passage of time.

보리밭

박화목(1924-2005, 아동 문학가, 시인)이 가사를 쓰고
윤용하(1922-1965, 작곡가)가 곡을 붙인 가곡.
어린이부터 어른까지 즐겨 부르는 한국인의 애창곡.
1952년 한국전쟁 당시 피난지인 부산에서 작곡되었다.
허전함을 희망으로 고양시키는 서정적 분위기가 인기의 비결이다.

Bo-Ri-Bart; The Barley Field

A Korean ariette of which *Park Hwa-Moak* (1924 - 2005,
Juvenile story writer, poet) wrote lyrics for and Yoon Yong-
Ha (1922–1965, songwriter) composed. Bo-Ri-Bart, is one
of the most beloved Korean songs that is sung by all age
groups; from children to adults.
This song was composed in Busan, the second largest city
in South Korea, where Koreans fled during the Korean
War in 1952. The lyrical mood of leading the listener from
emptiness to hope is the secret of the song's tremendous
popularity.

가을의 문턱에서 황량한 들판을 바라본다
하릴없이 돌아서는데 흙을 가득 메운 벌레들의 시신이 밟힌다
무릎 꿇고 애통의 눈물 뿌린다
다시 만나게 될 벌레들의 합창이 눈에 선하다

보리밭 사잇길로 걸어가면
뉘 부르는 소리 있어 나를 멈춘다

I see the empty field at the doorstep of Autumn
As I turn away from it idly, I step on deceased insects packed up in the soil
I go down on my knees, my tears are running down with grief
The chorus of summer insects I shall hear again is so vivid in my mind

When I stroll down sideways through Bo-Ri-Baat,
I stop as there is something calling me.

진주가 조개껍질 속에서 태어난다는 걸 믿지 않았어요

캄캄한 세상에서 당신을 발견하고 나서 그 이야기가 생각났어요

기적처럼 거기 계신 당신이

손잡아 이끄시네요

눈물 한 방울 떨어뜨리게 하시어

그 속에서 다른 세상을 보여주시네요

I never believed that a pearl is born from inside a shell

This story came to my mind after I found you in that pitch black world

How miraculous that you are there

You hold my hand to lead me to where you are

You let me shed a single drop of my tear

and present me with a whole new world within it.

고치 속에서

오래 살았지

고치인 줄도 잊었으니까

누군가 말하더군

당신이었을까

오래된 것과의 결별에 대해 들어본 적 있나요

어린 왕자처럼 사막에 떨어질지도 모른다죠

느닷없이 출구가 열렸고

어리둥절 나비 되어 낯선 세상으로 가는 중이야

I lived inside of a cocoon for a long time

So long…,

I even forgot it was a cocoon

Someone asked me

"Was it you?"

"Have you ever heard of breaking up with something old?"

"It could be akin to being dropped onto a desert like the Little Prince?"

All of a sudden, the exit was opened,

and I, bewildered, found myself to be a butterfly, flying to a strange world.